Wild Wes

Molly Dolly

SNIFFFFFF!

Mr. Humdinger

Cheese Louise

Ms. Honeycrisp

Henry Holt and Company, *Publishers since 1866*

Henry Holt® is a registered trademark of Macmillan Publishing Group, LLC.

120 Broadway, New York, NY 10271

mackids.com

Library of Congress Cataloging-in-Publication Data is available.

Our books may be purchased in bulk for promotional, educational, or business use.
Please contact your local bookseller or the Macmillan Corporate and
Premium Sales Department at (800) 221-7945 ext. 5442 or by email at
MacmillanSpecialMarkets@macmillan.com.

First Edition, 2021

Artwork created with graphite pencil on Strathmore drawing paper,
then scanned and colorized digitally.

Printed in China by RR Donnelley Asia Printing Solutions, Ltd.,
Dongguan City, Guangdong Province

ISBN 978-1-250-76599-4

1 3 5 7 9 10 8 6 4 2

From SEASON TO SEASON!

words and pictures by

Ethan Long

Christy Ottaviano Books

HENRY HOLT AND COMPANY

New York

Contents

WINTER

SPRING

What a Happy County!

The air is hot, the sky is clear, and it looks like the folks in Happy County are enjoying the fun days of summer.

Jumbo's Shrimps

PARK

The community pool is bustling. Look! Max just swam from one side of the pool to the other for the first time! Congratulations, Max!

POOL

There's Farmer Del riding his tractor . . .
and Dottie the Dog Walker . . . Ooh!
The Bright Brothers are testing out
their new invention, the Duo Wing 3000!
Whoosh!

Everyone is taking advantage
of this beautiful day!

LIBRA

9

At the Library

Don't you just love the library? It's especially fun when everyone is keeping up with their summer reading lists.

There are fiction books and nonfiction books. Fiction books contain stories that describe imaginary people and events. Nonfiction books are based on facts, real events, and real people.

Shelby loves to read information about whales and other sea life. Is that fiction or nonfiction?

clock

door

mobile

globe

Miss Beverly is keeping the library in tip-top shape. She makes sure everything is organized and running smoothly.

library card

computer

RESTROOM

sculpture

BOOK DROP

trash can

magazine

RANGER

floor

Everyone is welcome at the library, as long as they don't start a ruckus.

cart

rug

hat

book

table

ponytail

paper

11

Wild Wes!

Wes loves the library!

Woo-hoo!

He comes every week!

WOWEE!

SHHHH!

And every week, Wes goes wild.

What is THAT?

SHHHHH!

With every book he sees, he gets more and more excited.

YIPPEE!

YAHOO!

YOWZA!

SHHHH!

But, unfortunately, with every book he sees, he gets louder . . .

HEE HEE HEE!

SHHHH!

and louder . . .

HA HA HA HA HA HA HA!

SHHHHHHH!

and louder!

HARDY HAR HARRRRR!

SHHHHHHHHH!

Fortunately, Mom has a plan, just like she does every week.

Sometimes, a good book is all it takes.

The County in Action

jump
stretch
swing
walk
wander
dig
sing

Whew!

Take a look out the window. There is a lot of action happening.
Verbs are action words. Do you see any verbs that spark your interest?

fly

drip

ride

catch

throw

chase

climb

run

chop

camp

look

dab

swim

kick

read

rest

collect

fish

dance

hike

hide

hop

15

Back to School!

With summer winding down, it's time to go shopping for back-to-school supplies! Can you find what you're looking for?

NOTEBOOK **BLOWOUT!**

Thanks for Shopping!

EXIT

MAKE A SP

They're sold out of many items, so you'll have to pick out some other things. Are there any orange notebooks left? How about pencils? How many blue backpacks?

Manager Millie has a lot to do. Her lunch break is at noon. How many more hours does she have to wait?

RETURNS

20% off

The Decision

Alyssa is getting an early start today. It is 7:45. She leaves for school in one hour. What time will that be?

It's been five minutes and she can't decide what to wear.

She should start narrowing down her choices.

How much time has passed?

Which outfit should she choose?

Is this a good one?

Alyssa has been trying on outfits for thirty minutes.

How many minutes until she leaves for school?

Do you think she'll be ready on time?

Hmm.

Hmmmmmmm.

HMMMMMMMMMM.

Oh no! It's 8:40! The bus will be here in five minutes!

Time has run out! Which outfit will Alyssa wear?

School Is in Session

Oh my! She decided to wear them all!

I should start waking up a little earlier.

It's the first day of school, which means that summer is officially over. It's time for pencils! It's time for books! It's time for teachers with friendly looks!

Will has brought an apple for Ms. Honeycrisp. Can you find her?

Leaves, Leaves, Leaves!

Fall, also called autumn, is a wonderful time of year. The air becomes brisk and some birds start flying south for the winter. Maybe fall is hot where you live.

elm

maple

sycamore

oak

birch

white ash

It's a good time to sit around a campfire, take a hot-air balloon ride, or go apple picking! It's also fun to watch the leaves change. This neighborhood has lots of trees. Which tree is your favorite?

black gum

chestnut

beech

cedar

sweet gum

spruce

dogwood

apple

Do you know which of these trees produces acorns? Hint: Look for the squirrels!

cherry

The Maze Craze!

This corn maze will leave you in a daze! There are so many different ways, it might take you days!

I'm a Little Snowflake
(to the tune of "I'm a Little Teapot")

I'm a little snow burst,
cold and white!
Six feet of snow
is such a delight!

My back hurts.

I'm a little blizzard,
blowing with glee.
Your cute little plow
is no match for me.

But I just bought it!

I'm a little snowdrift . . .

Okay. You can stop singing now.

Snowflakes

Experts say that no two snowflakes are exactly the same, but it looks like we will get lucky today. Can you find matching snowflakes in this flurry?

Molly and Dolly Build an Igloo

Deep Winter

house

heart

hill

snow
angels

dog

tongue

pile

shovel

flower

hat

coffee

Just because it's winter doesn't mean you have to stay inside. There are many things to do when it's cold out. You can have a snowball fight, ride a sled, and make a snow angel! It's also the perfect time to go ice-skating!

smoke

truck

tree

Snowman

ladder

ice skates

fishing rod

hot chocolate

igloo

skis

snowblower

fence

snowball

scarf

sled

Get outside before the snow melts!

snowshoes

ramp

Spring Forward!

Wow! It's spring already, and the snow has all melted. There's a sweet smell in the air! In fact, there are many sweet smells in the air. How many different gardens can you see?

Can you also find ten things that are wrong in this picture?

Be the Bee

Mr. Humdinger is admiring his beautiful flower garden.
It is a sight to behold!

The bees love it, too!
Look! It's time to collect the nectar!

The pollen from the flower rubs on the bee's body.

Then, the bee carries the pollen to another flower to deposit it onto the stigma.

The stigma is that middle part of the flower that sticks out.

Spring Training

The baseball season can't start until all the players and coaches report for spring training. This is the time to get in shape and practice their skills for the upcoming season.

Monkey Mantle is signing autographs for his adoring fans, Manager Tammi Lasorda is giving a funny interview, and Sunny the Mascot is entertaining the audience.

bees

flowers

food truck

bleachers

program

binoculars

TINA TUSKER IS YOUR COMMISH!

MARY'S DAIRY

PeeWee's POPSICLES

EWE-HA

cleat

lawn mower

baseball

football

bubble gum

rock

fly

glove

saliva

infield dirt

helmet

batting rings

gopher

net

batting cage

beach ball

bucket

baseball bat

vampire bat

Cloud Types

It looks like today ended up being a little cloudy. A cloud is a collection of tiny droplets of water. The droplets are so small and light that they can float in the air.

Sssonny Sssnakerton loves the clouds because they bring lots of rain.

Sssssensssational!

There are different cloud formations,
which vary due to altitude and density.

Cirrus

Cirrus clouds are wispy clouds that look like tufts of hair. They are found at high altitudes and are some of the whitest clouds in the sky.

Cumulus

Cumulus clouds have flat bases with large fluffy puffs that look like cotton balls. They may be only 2,000 feet above the ground.

Stratus

Stratus clouds are the lowest-lying clouds, can be either gray or white colored, and can sometimes appear as mist or fog.

It's Summer Again!

In the blink of an eye, a year has gone by! Time for swimming, fishing, and having a good old time under the sun.

Be sure to wear your sunscreen and watch out for paper biplanes crossing the sky. Before you know it, it will be autumn again.

Living from season to season is the way life goes here in Happy County. Maybe your seasons are a little different where you live, but we know they bring just as much joy.

So long!

LIBRA